HOW TO ENJOY THIS BOOK

Scratch and Sniff

To release the fragrance in the rose, the
strawberry jam, the pine needles, the peach,
the dill pickle, and the chocolate cookie,
scratch each sticker with your fingernail and
then smell the sticker.

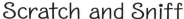

A GOLDEN BOOK • NEW YORK

Copyright © 1971, renewed 1999 by Random House, Inc. All rights reserved under International and Pan-American Copyright Conventions. Published in the United States by Golden Books, an imprint of Random House Children's Books, a division of Random House, Inc., New York, NY 10019, and simultaneously in Canada by Random House of Canada Limited, Toronto. Golden Books, A Golden Book, and the G colophon are registered trademarks of Random House, Inc. Originally published by Western Publishing Company, Inc., in 1971. Library of Congress Control Number: 2003104183

ISBN: 0-375-82644-0

www.goldenbooks.com

MANUFACTURED IN THE UNITED STATES OF AMERICA   First Random House Edition 2004
10 9 8 7 6 5 4 3 2 1

Little Bunny Follows His Nose

By Katherine Howard
Illustrated by J. P. Miller

One day after lunch, Little Bunny's mother said, "Why don't you go out and play?"
"But what can I do?" asked Little Bunny.
"You'll find something," said his mother. "Just follow your nose."

"Follow my nose," thought Little Bunny as he went outside. "Follow my nose—follow my nose." Hop, hop, hop, he followed his nose up a hill. Over the hill was a field full of flowers and buzzing bees.

"What are you doing, Little Bunny?" buzzed his friend Bee.
"I'm following my nose," said Little Bunny. "What smells so nice?"

"It's the roses," buzzed Bee. "I think they have one of the nicest smells in the world. Now if you'll excuse me, I must get back to the hive to make more honey."
Away he buzzed.

Little Bunny leaned close to the rose and sniffed. "Mm-m-m," he said. "Bee was right. It is a nice smell."

Here is a rose for you to smell.
Scratch and sniff. Isn't it nice?

Hop, hop, hop, Little Bunny followed his nose down the hill.
"What are you doing, Little Bunny?" asked his friend Mouse.
"I'm following my nose," said Little Bunny. "What are you doing?"
"I'm picking strawberries," said Mouse. "My mother is making
strawberry jam."

"I'll help you," said Little Bunny.
Together they carried the strawberries to Mouse's house.

The kitchen was filled with a wonderful aroma. "What smells so delicious?" asked Little Bunny.

"I'm making jam," said Mouse's mother. "It's too hot to taste right now, but if you come here, you may smell it."

Little Bunny took a big sniff of the strawberry jam. "Mm-m-m," he said, "it smells wonderful."

"Well, Little Bunny," said Mouse's mother, "tomorrow, when the jam is cool, I'll give you a jar of your very own."

Here is a spoonful of Mother Mouse's special strawberry jam. Scratch and sniff. Doesn't it smell wonderful?

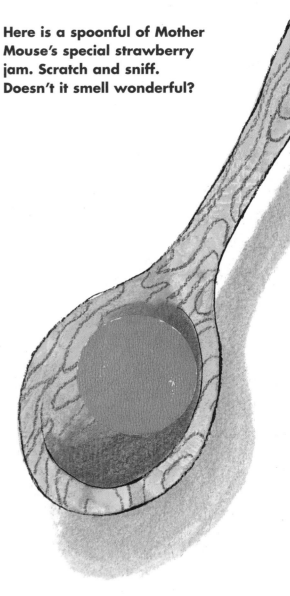

Hop, hop, hop, Little Bunny followed his nose into the forest.

"What are you doing here, Little Bunny?" asked his friend Squirrel.

"I'm following my nose," said
Little Bunny. "What smells so green
and foresty?"

"It's the pine needles," said Squirrel.

Little Bunny put his nose near the pine needles and sniffed. "The smell reminds me of winter," he said.

These pine needles are for you to smell. Scratch and sniff. Do they remind you of anything special?

Hop, hop, hop, Little Bunny followed his nose across a big field to a clump of green trees.

"What are you doing here?" asked his friend Bird.

"I'm following my nose," said Little Bunny. "What smells so nice?"

"The peaches," said Bird. "They are not quite ripe yet, but you can smell them."

Little Bunny took a big sniff. "Mm-m-m, they smell fantastic," he said.

"Come back next week," said Bird, "and you can pick some to eat."

Here is a peach for you. Scratch and sniff. Do you think it smells fantastic?

Hop, hop, hop, Little Bunny followed his nose to a vegetable garden.
"What are you doing here?" asked his friend Raccoon.

"I'm following my nose," said Little Bunny. "What are you doing here?"

"Picking cucumbers," said Raccoon. "My mother is making them into dill pickles."

"I'll help you," said Little Bunny. "I've never tasted a dill pickle in my whole life."

They carried the cucumbers to Raccoon's house. The kitchen was filled with a sharp smell.

"Mommy," said Raccoon, "Little Bunny has never tasted a dill pickle."

"Then he must try one of mine," said Raccoon's mother, and she gave him one.

Little Bunny sniffed the pickle. "My," he said, "it certainly smells good." He took a bite. "And it tastes as good as it smells."

"Come over next week, Little Bunny," said Raccoon's mother, "and I will give you a jar of freshly made pickles for your mother."

Here is one of Mother Raccoon's dill pickles. Scratch and sniff. Doesn't that smell good?

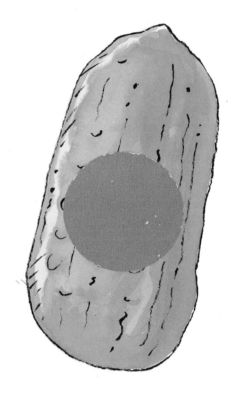

It was getting late, so Little Bunny followed his nose straight home. There was a wonderful smell coming through the door. "I wonder what that is," he said to himself.

When he walked into the kitchen, he found out. His mother had been baking cookies. He took a big sniff. "Aha!" he said. "I smell my favorite kind of cookie—chocolate chip."

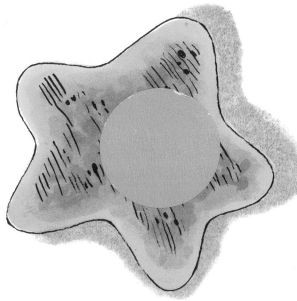

This chocolate chip cookie
is for you. Scratch and sniff.
Is it your favorite, too?

After dinner, Little Bunny ate four chocolate chip cookies and drank two big glasses of milk. Then he was tired, so he took a bath, put on his pajamas, and climbed into bed.

Soon his mother came to kiss him good night. "Good night, Mommy," said Little Bunny. "I had a wonderful time today, just following my nose."